After
HAPPILY
—EVER—
AFTER

Mr. Giant
and the Beastly Baron

After Happily Ever After is published by Stone Arch Books
A Capstone Imprint
1710 Roe Crest Drive
North Mankato, Minnesota 56003
www.capstonepub.com

First published by Orchard Books, a division of Hachette Children's Books
338 Euston Road, London NW1 3BH, United Kingdom

Library of Congress Cataloging-in-Publication Data is available
on the Library of Congress website.

ISBN-13: 978-1-4342 -7949-1 (hardcover)
ISBN-13: 978-1-4342-7955-2 (paperback)

Summary: Even though the giant is nice, he must be scary to save himself
and his friends from the mean baron.

Designer: Russell Griesmer
Photo Credits: ShutterStock/Maaike Boot, 4, 5, 51

Printed in China.
092013   007737LEOS14

After
HAPPILY
—EVER—
AFTER

Mr. Giant
and the Beastly Baron

by TONY BRADMAN
illustrated by SARAH WARBURTON

 STONE ARCH BOOKS®
a capstone imprint

So Jack and his mother lived
happily ever after, leaving
Mr. Giant in a tough spot.
And then ...

It was a lovely morning, and the sun shone on Mr. Giant as he walked into the village to do his weekly shopping. He was careful where he put his boots, of course. But he didn't need to worry. The villagers weren't scared. They were pleased to see him.

"Hey there, Mr. Giant!" people called happily. "How are things?"

"Couldn't be better, thanks," said
Mr. Giant with a shy smile.

In fact, he could hardly believe how well things were going for him these days. He still had occasional nightmares about Jack, and hoped he would never, ever meet him again.

But he was also grateful to the little rascal. Jack had made him think about the kind of life he was living.

The truth was that up there in his castle, Mr. Giant had been rather bored and lonely. He'd had no hobbies, no interests, and no friends. Everybody had always run off screaming as soon as they heard him growl, "Fee, fi, fo, fum …"

A week in the Fairy Tale Clinic for Recovering Villains had made all the difference. He learned that he could change if he wanted to. Mr. Giant had promised himself he would give up being nasty and violent forever.

He decided to leave his castle and moved to a lovely village on the far side of the forest. Mr. Giant settled down to live a peaceful, happy life. The villagers were nice to him right from the start, and he soon made plenty of friends.

He joined the Village Social Club and
took up stamp collecting.

Now the only problems he had were small ones. His cottage was a bit cramped, and he didn't think he would ever get used to eating such tiny portions of food.

On this particular afternoon, Mr. Giant finished his shopping and set off for home. But suddenly he heard shouting and went back to find out what was happening. He hid behind an enormous, old oak tree and peered out.

A short, plump man with a mean face was standing on one of the benches outside the village tavern. He was shouting at a group of villagers, who were being pushed around by a group of tough-looking soldiers.

"I'm Baron Beastly, your new lord and master," the short man yelled. "And I'm doubling — no, tripling — your taxes. You have until next week to pay me."

"What if we can't?" said somebody. "We don't have that much money."

"You'd better find it, then," snapped
Baron Beastly, glaring at the villagers.
"Otherwise, I'll get my soldiers to burn down
your pretty little village. And don't think I
won't do it, either. I'm beastly by nature as
well as by name."

Mr. Giant felt anger boiling up inside him as he listened. "Fee, fi, fo, fum …" he murmured.

Now Baron Beastly and his beastly men were marching out of the village, and Mr. Giant almost followed them. He had a vision of just what he would do.

Then Mr. Giant realized what he was thinking and felt ashamed. He had made a promise not to be like that ever again, and he was determined not to break that promise.

Once he started behaving badly, he was worried he wouldn't be able to stop.

That evening, the villagers held a crisis meeting in the village hall. Mr. Giant squeezed in with everybody else and listened to them argue about what to do.

"We need somebody who can stand up to Baron Beastly," said one of the villagers eventually. "Somebody who could really scare the pants off him."

"What about you, Mr. Giant?" said the village baker. "You're a big guy. I bet you could be pretty scary if you put your mind to it."

"No, count me out. I don't do that kind of thing," muttered Mr. Giant. He could feel everybody staring at him, and he blushed.

"Oh, fair enough," said the baker, raising his eyebrows. A sigh of disappointment rustled through the hall. "It'll have to be Plan B, then."

Plan B was simple. The villagers put together all the money they had, even their savings and the coins from their children's piggy banks.

That wasn't enough, so they sold their
jewelry and their best animals.

Mr. Giant chipped in with everything he had too. He wondered if the villagers were annoyed with him. But they seemed very thankful for his money, and were just as nice to him as ever, which made him feel all the more guilty, of course.

"It looks like we've hit the target," said the baker. "We'll give the money to Baron Beastly tomorrow and our troubles will be over."

Their troubles weren't over, though. Early the next day, Baron Beastly marched into the village with his men. He shouted at the villagers, demanding the money, and they handed it over.

Baron Beastly laughed and did a little victory dance.

"There you go. That wasn't hard, was it?" he said with a smirk. "And seeing as you're so good at raising money, I'll be back next week for the same amount."

"Next week?!" squeaked the baker. The crowd behind him groaned. "We won't be able to come up with a penny more. The village is totally broke."

"Well, that's not my problem," said Baron Beastly, shrugging. "Either you find the cash, or you'll be homeless this winter. It's up to you."

The villagers held another crisis meeting that afternoon, but nobody could think of a solution.

Mr. Giant listened to them arguing, then sadly trudged back to his little cottage.

He sat alone, his huge head in his big
hands. His mind was in a whirl.

He wanted to help his friends and
save the village, but he couldn't break his
promise. It was all too difficult to think
about. Only somebody really clever would
be able to work out what he should do.

Then suddenly it hit him. He knew exactly the right person, although the thought of meeting Jack again sent shivers of fear down his spine. But he would have to do it if he wanted to save the village.

So Mr. Giant wrote a letter.

A couple of days later, there was a knock on Mr. Giant's door.

"Hey there, big guy!" said Jack. "Great to see you again! How are things?"

"Not so good, actually," murmured Mr. Giant. "I need your help."

A nervous Mr. Giant invited Jack in, and they talked over tea and cupcakes.

"What are you worried about?" asked Jack at last. "You should scare the pants off this Baron Beastly guy, then carry on being the new you."

"But do you think I can do both?" said Mr. Giant. "What if I can't control myself? What if I slip back into my old ways and start being nasty again?"

"You can do anything if you set your mind to it," said Jack. "That's how a little guy like me managed to run rings round a big guy like you, anyway."

"Really?" said Mr. Giant, offering him another cupcake. "I see what you mean."

So a week later, when Baron Beastly and his men marched into the village to collect the taxes, they got a nasty surprise.

A colossal shadow fell over them and Mr. Giant put on his scariest face.

He roared and stamped his massive,
great boots. His huge voiced boomed out,
    "Fee, fi, fo, fum! Look out Baron Beastly,
here I come!"

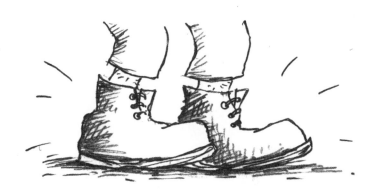

Baron Beastly and his men ran screaming out of the village.

For a brief moment Mr. Giant felt like following them to finish the job. But he didn't. He thought of Jack instead, and kept himself firmly under control.

Baron Beastly and his men never, ever returned to the village. In fact, the baron was so terrified of Mr. Giant, he sent all the villagers' money back.

And to thank his friend, the baker made
Mr. Giant an absolutely enormous cake.

So, against all the odds, the villagers and Mr. Giant managed to live HAPPILY EVER AFTER!

ABOUT THE AUTHOR

Tony Bradman writes for children of all ages. He is particularly well known for his top-selling Dilly the Dinosaur series. His other titles include the Happily Ever After series, *The Orchard Book of Heroes and Villains*, and *The Orchard Book of Swords*, *Sorcerers*, and *Superheroes*. Tony lives in South East London.

ABOUT THE ILLUSTRATOR

Sarah Warburton is a rising star in children's books. She is the illustrator of the Rumblewick series, which has been very well received at an international level. The series spans across both picture books and fiction. She has also illustrated nonfiction titles and the Happily Ever After series. She lives in Bristol, England, with her young baby and husband.

GLOSSARY

beastly (BEEST-lee) — horrible or unkind

colossal (kuh-LOSS-uhl) — extremely large

cramped (KRAMPT) — very full

crisis (KRYE-siss) — a turning point or decision point

murmured (MUR-murd) — talked quietly

muttered (MUHT-urd) — spoke in a low, unclear way

rascal (RASS-kuhl) — someone who is very mischievous

taxes (TAKS-ez) — money that people and businesses must pay in order to support a government

trudged (TRUHJD) — walked slowly and with effort

vision (VIZH-uhn) — something that you imagine or dream about

DISCUSSION QUESTIONS

1. In the original story, Mr. Giant was a bully. However, he worked hard and changed his ways. Were you surprised by his new lifestyle? Explain your answer.

2. Do you think it was a good idea for Mr. Giant to scare Beastly Baron and his group? Why or why not?

3. Why do you think Beastly Baron was so mean?

WRITING PROMPTS

1. When Mr. Giant needed help, he called Jack. Write about a person you would call if you needed help or advice.

2. Write a letter to Mr. Giant thanking him for getting rid of Beastly Baron.

3. Add another chapter to the story explaining what Beastly Baron is doing now. Is he still mean or did he change his ways?

THE FUN DOESN'T STOP HERE!

DISCOVER MORE AT...
WWW.CAPSTONEKIDS.COM